Spud and Smud
the little orphans
by
Jason Quinn

PHOENIX PRESS LTD

Published 2023
First Edition
PHOENIX PRESS LTD
www.newhavenpublishingltd.com
newhavenpublishing@gmail.com

Cover Art © Jason Quinn

Cover Design © Pete Cunliffe

PHOENIX
— PRESS —

"It's okay to be afraid of stuff. Scares are good."

Smud

"No it isn't. Scares stink."

Spud

Welcome to Hilltop Orphanage,
home to Spud and Smud.

Spud and Smud are playing hide
and seek in the woods...

One, two, seven, fifty-four, five hundred!
I'm coming to get you, Smud!

This is Spud and Smud's guardian.
They call him Guardian.

Spud! Smud! Diiinner time!
It's your favourite... liver!

Guardian! Guardian!
HELP!!!

Well? What is it, Spud?

It... it's Smud.
He's lost
in the woods...

I looked everywhere...
I think he must be dead.

The whole village searched for Smud...

They searched until the sun went down...

Yes, Constable, this is he... Ah... most unfortunate. No... don't be silly, we'll be happy to identify the body.... yes... ta-ta for now.

The police have found a body in an abandoned mine. Let's see if it's our boy, Smud.

sob!

I'm fwightened. I don't want to see Smud all dead.

There's nothing to be scared of. It will be just the same as if he was alive. Only he won't be moving about. Now, come on.

... Smud is littler than him, and he didn't have a funny hat, or an axe.

Now, now Spud. You're in what we call denial. The killer probably gave him the hat as a present. Now, let's get home for us tea.

Look, this is all very touching, but does this cadaver belong to you, or are we just playing spin the bottle?

The boy may be right.
Here have some liver
for your pains.

Liver?

Liver?
I work in
a morgue.
I've got
liver
coming out
of my ears,
you cheap
fink!

Step lively, lads.
I'll rustle us up some liver
for us supper.

In the kitchen...

Donner und
blitzen!

Hey, Spud!
Hey, Guardian!
Where were you?
I had to make my
own dish-dish!
Want some?

Smud! We thought you
were dead!

Don't be
daft! I was
playing
hide and
seek.
I win...
again!

You selfish creature!
We are sick with the
worry! I will break
my stick on you!

THWAK

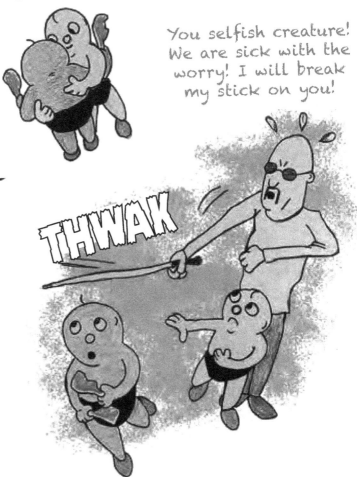

Morning has broken at Hilltop Orphanage...

Spud! Smud! Breakfast's ready!

I've made your favourite... liver. Now, eat up, we've got a lot to do this morning.

Yaaay! I love it when there's lots to do!

Oh, no... he's going to make us do something horrid, like sweep the chimney, or unblock his toilet.

There's nothing to worry about. We're going to get your birthday present! Happy birthday boys!

You mean we're going to have a real birthday? With a real present?

Wa-hey! I love presents!

So what is it, Guardian? Tell us! Go on!

You'll find out soon enough, lads!

This is your present!
A trip to the barbers!
Your hair's getting out
of hand. You look like a
pair of beatniks!

So, what will
it be, lads?

I'll have the works,
please, Rabbity! Oh,
and something for
the weekend too!

Be careful
with those!

There we go!
You looks
super smarts!

SNIP

SNIP

Later, back at the Orphanage...

Spud! Why are you crying? It's our birthday! The bestest day in the world!

That's why I'm crying. None of our friends came to our party!

That's cos we never invited anyone! Let's ask Guardian to invite Bonnie and Clive to come for cake!

Guardian! Can Bonnie and Clive come to our party?

I bet he says no.

Sigh! As if I don't have enough on my plate!

Hallo?! Yes... Bonnie and Clive are invited to a party at Hilltop Orphanage, along with your good self too. Now, turn left at the station and go past Boots the chemist. At the brow of the hill turn right and go past the United Reform church and take the footpath on the left.

Then climb the style and cross the fallow field. Watch out for the muddy puddles. Then you'll come to a stone wall. Vault over it and you'll find yourself in the deep, dark woods. Don't veer off the path or you'll fall in the bog. Stick to it until you get to the graveyard and you reach the cliff path.

... Oh, what's that? Wrong number? You don't know Bonnie and Clive? Ah... no... my apologies... and yes, by all means do come anyway. You have the directions.

Well? Are Bonnie and Clive coming?

Not exactly, no. But you're going to make some new friends. The Sarapatis are coming!

They won't be.

Oh, boy! Who are the Sarapatis?

I bet they're horrid!

DING DONG

Wa-hoo! That'll be them! I'll get it!

Smud, Spud! You just missed out on birthday cake and jelly. It was lovely. Never mind, there's still some jaggery left!

Did you have fun with the baby? Was he a delight?

Don't say anything, Smud.

We did not have fun! You're a big fat liar, Mr. Sarapati. That baby is not fun. He's a misery.

I know he is a disheartening baby. But you have all eternity to get used to him. Your Guardian won him in a game of beggar your neighbour.

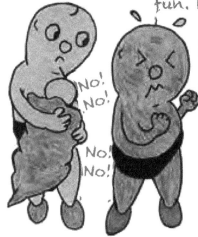

No! No!

No! No!

Goodnight, Spud. You never know, the baby might be fun when he grows up.

I don't think so! Goodnight!

No! No! No! No!

Goodnight, boys. I'm glad you like your birthday baby.

One fine morning...

Smud! Spud!
Get down
here!
Now!

The fridge is kaput!
I need you to dig a
hole to keep the wine
and meat cool for my
army friends tonight!

Yaaay! We love digging!

What if we fall in
the hole and die?
Digging's dangerous.

Later...

Smud, it's
bedtime,
where are
you going?

To spy on
Guardian
and
his army
friends,
come on!

Guardian's friends
used to be shoulders.
What if they catch us
and shoot us?

Ha! Imagine
if they did!
What a hoot!
Don't worry,
we'll be dead
sneaky!

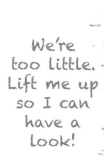

Stop wiggling, Spud!

Smud! There's something out there, in the dark!

It's just Invalid! But where's the baby?

Who cares? We can stand on his chair and look in the window!

Tonight, after years of living in the shadows, we see a new dawn. May I introduce the fuhrer's favourite physician, comedian, and practitioner of magic... Doctor Lachen...

Thank you! Tonight, thanks to the wonders of National Socialist science and Satanic rituals, we shall transform this dispiriting infant into Herr Hitler himself! Boom-Boom!

Come on lads, fun's over. Let's pop in and see Pete the butcher.

Well, boys, all's well that ends well, eh?

Children, we aren't Nasties. We're starting up a drama club. We were just playing. We were good, ja?

No, it isn't! You're a Nasty and your nasties turned the baby into Baby Hitler!

Guardian,
I'm glad
you're not
a Nasty.

And we
think
you're a
great actor.

Thank you boys.
That's enough
chatter.
Night-night.

Nein
Nein! Nein! Nein!

Next morning...

Guardian, why aren't you eating your liver?

I'm too nervous, Smud. I've got a date this afternoon. With a woman.

Why do I have to sit next to Invalid? He stinks?

Later...

I don't know what to wear.

Wear your Nasty uniform. You look great in it.

Women don't like Nasty uniforms. Wear your Sunday best.

And so Guardian dressed in his Sunday best and waited for his date to arrive.

This scent makes you smell like our toilet.

DING DONG!

Oh, dear... That'll be her!

ZOOOOOM

Waah-hooo! I'll get it! I'll get it! I'll get it!

God says 'do handstands.'

Wooh! Look at me! Champion handstander!

Ooh! I feel dizzy.

Well done. God will shower you in kisses.

Wowza!

Yuk!

God says 'throw Invalid off roof and watch him fly.'

Go on. Don't make God angry.

What a great idea!

No, Smud! It's not allowed.

Now, have you all had fun while we were out?

Yes, we looked after the baby boys.

That's good, darlings, because we are all going to live together, aren't we Guardie?

That's right. Galina and I are to be married.

Now we can play together for ever and ever and ever.

Oh, boy!

I don't want Guardian to marry Galina. I don't like Grainne and Ainne.

Shut your mouth, Spud! I love them and I'm going to marry them!

Cut it out you two! It's late.

I'm Guardian's Best Man. I'm going to get him to the church on time. And you are going to keep your cousin Fhingus, out of trouble.

Wow! We've got a cousin!

We're not cousins. You're orphans. You don't have a family.

I'm going to give my brother a makeover. Wish me luck!

He's gonna make Guardian handsome!

The local chapel...

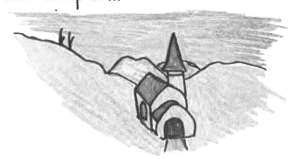

Later...

Let's play Angry God,
Loving God.

Nobody's playing anything!
Go to sleep!

No, it's too late.
We'll get in trouble!

Guardie, stop making nois
We're trying to make love

I'll play. It sounds copacetic!

You dodged a bullet
there, hermano!
She's insatiable!

Early morning...
All my life, it's been the same old story. Gardener always takes whatever he thinks I want, It's not fair. I'm a failier. That's what I am. A big fat, failier.
'Scuze! You're blocking the way and I'm running late!

Oi! What's the rush? Mind the brew, it's hot!

Soz! No time to chat! I'm off to see my girlfriend!

Girlfriend? What girlfriend? You know she'll only break your heart!

No she won't! She's not like that! She's my half banana!

Later that evening...

Spud is not important. He can barely think. Tell them, hubby o'mine.

It's like this. We're just starting out on this adventure called marriage, and we feel you and the boys should move out. And if you'd take the girls and Fhingus, that would be cool too.

But...

Ah-ah, no buts. I'll even throw in the keys to the camper van. It's still got two months on the M.O.T. Now you can't get much fairer than that, can you?

Well... I...

Meanwhile...

Come on, I want you to meet my family. Don't be shy. They'll love you.

Oooh! Look what the cat dragged in!

Guys, there's someone I want you all to meet!

GRRRR! How dare you? She is the love of my life and I WILL marry her!

Come on, Bonnie. We're running away! Goodbye... For ever!!

Spud! Wait! Don't go!

Well, that's one less burden for you to worry about!

Good riddance to the soppy little twit!

That does it! Smud, you and Fhingus and the girls go and find Spud. I need a word with this pair!

Ah... good news! Gardener and Galina have decided to go away on a long honeymoon. You just missed them.

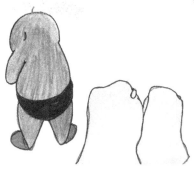

That's great, Guardian, but we can't find Spud anywhere!

And so, Guardian and Smud set out on a long road trip, looking for Spud and his fiancée. Will they find them? That remains to be seen...

Most definitely not the end!

What do you think it means, 'not the end'?

Maybe we're supposed to do something?

I'm not doing anything except catching up on my Zs.

Fasten your seatbelt!   You fasten yours!

KER-UNCH!

That doesn't sound good.

It's flat! What have I told you about leaving bottles around?

Don't worry, Guardian. I've got an idea.

It's that stupid hole you two made! And we've smashed all my wines and meats!

Don't worry, Guardian. We can always look for Spud tomorrow.

GREAT!
Now the car
battery's kaput!
I can't see a
thing!

How exciting!

Still not quite the end...

Ingram Content Group UK Ltd.
Milton Keynes UK
UKHW050341070323
418151UK00028B/363